The Surrender Tree

Poems of Cuba's Struggle for Freedom

Margarita Engle

Henry Holt and Company
New York

For Curtis, Victor, and Nicole, with love

AND

in memory of my maternal great-grandparents, Cuban
guajiros *who survived the turmoil described in this book:*

PEDRO EULOGIO SALUSTIANO URÍA Y TRUJILLO

(1859–1915)

ANA DOMINGA DE LA PEÑA Y MARRERO

DE TRUJILLO

(1872–1965)

Henry Holt and Company, LLC
Publishers since 1866
175 Fifth Avenue
New York, New York 10010
www.HenryHoltKids.com

Henry Holt® is a registered trademark of Henry Holt and Company, LLC.
Copyright © 2008 by Margarita Engle
All rights reserved.
Distributed in Canada by H. B. Fenn and Company Ltd.

Library of Congress Cataloging-in-Publication Data
Engle, Margarita.
The surrender tree / Margarita Engle.
p.   cm.
ISBN-13: 978-0-8050-8674-4
ISBN-10: 0-8050-8674-9
1. Cuba—History—1810–1899—Juvenile poetry.   2. Children's poetry, American.   I. Title.
PS3555.N4254S87 2008   811'.54—dc22   2007027591

First Edition—2008
Book designed by Lilian Rosenstreich
Printed in February 2009 in the United States of America by R.R. Donnelley and Sons
Company, Harrisonburg, Virginia, on acid-free paper. ∞

10 9 8 7 6 5 4 3 2

On October 10, 1868, a handful of Cuban plantation owners freed their slaves and declared independence from Spain. Throughout the next three decades of war, nurses hid in jungle caves, healing the wounded with medicines made from wild plants.

On February 16, 1896, Cuban peasants were ordered to leave their farms and villages. They were given eight days to reach "reconcentration camps" near fortified cities. Anyone found in the countryside after eight days would be killed.

My great-grandparents were two of the refugees.

Yo sé los nombres extraños
De las yerbas y las flores,
Y de mortales engaños,
Y de sublimes dolores.

I know the strange names
Of the herbs and the flowers,
And deadly betrayals,
And sacred sorrows.

—JOSÉ MARTÍ,
from *Versos Sencillos*
(*Simple Verses*), 1891

Contents

PART
One

The Names of the Flowers
1850–51

Rosa

Some people call me a child-witch,
but I'm just a girl who likes to watch
the hands of the women
as they gather wild herbs and flowers
to heal the sick.

I am learning the names of the cures
and how much to use,
and which part of the plant,
petal or stem, root, leaf, pollen, nectar.

Sometimes I feel like a bee making honey—
a bee, feared by all, even though the wild bees
of these mountains in Cuba
are stingless, harmless, the source
of nothing but sweet, golden food.

Rosa

We call them wolves,
but they're just wild dogs,
howling mournfully—
lonely runaways,
like *cimarrones,*
the runaway slaves who survive
in deep forest, in caves of sparkling crystal
hidden behind waterfalls,
and in secret villages
protected by magic

protected by words—
tales of guardian angels,
mermaids, witches,
giants, ghosts.

Rosa

When the slavehunter brings back
runaways he captures,
he receives seventeen silver *pesos*
per *cimarrón*,
unless the runaway is dead.
Four *pesos* is the price of an ear,
shown as proof that the runaway slave
died fighting, resisting capture.

The sick and injured
are brought to us, to the women,
for healing.

When a runaway is well again,
he will either choose to go back to work
in the coffee groves and sugarcane fields,
or run away again
secretly, silently, alone.

Lieutenant Death

My father keeps a diary.
It is required
by the Holy Brotherhood of Planters,
who hire him to catch runaway slaves.

I watch my father write the numbers
and nicknames of slaves he captures.
He does not know their real names.

When the girl-witch heals a wounded runaway,
the *cimarrón* is punished, and sent back to work.
Even then, many run away again,
or kill themselves.
But then my father chops each body
into four pieces, and locks each piece in a cage,
and hangs the four cages on four branches
of the same tree.

That way, my father tells me, the other slaves
will be afraid to kill themselves.
He says they believe
a chopped, caged spirit cannot fly away
to a better place.

Rosa

I love the sounds
of the jungle at night.

When the barracoon
where we sleep
has been locked,
I hear the music
of crickets, tree frogs, owls,
and the whir of wings
as night birds fly,
and the song of *un sinsonte,*
a Cuban mockingbird,
the magical creature
who knows how to sing
many songs all at once,
sad and happy,
captive and free . . .

songs that help me sleep
without nightmares,
without dreams.

Rosa

The names of the villages where runaways hide
are *Mira-Cielo,* Look-at-the-Sky
and *Silencio,* Silence
Soledad, Loneliness
La Bruja, The Witch. . . .

I watch the slavehunter as he writes his numbers,
while his son,
the boy we secretly call Lieutenant Death,
helps him make up big lies.

The slavehunter and his boy agree to exaggerate,
in order to make their work
sound more challenging,
so they will seem like heroes
who fight against armies with guns,
instead of just a few frightened, feverish, hungry,
escaped slaves,
armed only with wooden spears,
and secret hopes.

Lieutenant Death

When I call the little witch
a witch-girl, my father corrects me—
Just little witch is enough, he says, don't add girl,
or she'll think she's human, like us.

A pile of ears sits on the ground,
waiting to be counted.

This boy has a wound,
my father tells the witch.
Heal him.

The little witch stares at my arm, torn by wolves,
and I grin,
not because I have to be healed by a slave-witch,
but because it is comforting to know
that wild dogs
can be called wolves,
to make them sound
more dangerous,
making me seem
truly brave.

Rosa

The slavehunter and his son
both stay away during the rains,
which last six months, from May
through October.

In November he returns with his boy,
whose scars have faded.

This time they have their own pack of dogs,
huge ones,
taught to follow only the scent
of a barefoot track,
the scent of bare skin from a slave
who eats cornmeal and yams,

never the scent of a rich man on horseback,
after his huge meal of meat, fowl, fruit,
coffee, chocolate, and cream.

Lieutenant Death

We bring wanted posters from the cities,
with pictures drawn by artists,
pictures of men with filed teeth
and women with tribal scars,
new slaves
who somehow managed to run away
soon after escaping from ships
that landed secretly, at night,
on hidden beaches.

I look at the pictures
and wonder
how all these slaves
from faraway places
find their way
to this wilderness
of caves and cliffs,
wild mountains, green forest, little witches.

Rosa

After Christmas, on January 6,
the Festival of Three Kings Day,
we line up and walk, one by one,
to the thrones where our owner and his wife
are seated, like a king and queen
from a story.

They give us small gifts of food.
We bow down, and bless them,
our gift of words freely given
on this day of hope,
when we feel like we have
nothing to lose.

Rosa

The nicknames of runaways
keep us busy at night,
in the barracoons, where we whisper.

All the other young girls agree with me
that *Domingo* is a fine nickname,
because it means Sunday, our only half day of rest,
and *Dios Da* is even better,
because it means God Gives,
and *El Médico* is wonderful—
who would not be proud
to be known as The Doctor?

La Madre is the nickname
that fascinates us most—
The Mother—a woman, and not just a runaway,
but the leader of her own secret village,
free, independent, uncaptured—
for thirty-seven
magical years!

Lieutenant Death

My father captures some who pretend
they don't know their owners' names,
or the names of the plantations
where they belong.

They must want to be sold
to someone new.

They must hope that if they are sold here,
near the steamy, jungled wilderness,
they will be close to the caves,
and the waterfalls,
and witches.

My father brings the same runaways back,
over and over.

I don't understand why they never give up!
Why don't they lose hope?

Rosa

People imagine that all slaves are dark,
but the indentured Chinese slaves run away too,
into the mangrove swamps,
where they can fish, and spear frogs,
and hunt crocodiles by placing a hat on a stick
to make it look like a man.

The crocodile jumps straight up,
out of the gloomy water,
and snatches the hat,
while a noose of rope made from vines
tightens around the beast's green, leathery neck.

I would be afraid to live in the swamps.
People say there are *güijes*,
small, wrinkled, green mermaids
with long, red hair and golden combs . . .
mermaids who would lure me
down into the swamp depths . . .
mermaids who would drag me into watery caves,
where they would turn me into a mermaid too . . .
frog-green, and tricky.

Rosa

The slavehunter comes
with an offer.

He wants to buy me
so I can travel
with his horsemen
and his huge dogs
and his strange son
into the wild places
where wounded captives
can be healed
so they won't die.

The price
of a healed man
is much higher
than the price
of an ear.

Rosa

My owner refuses.
He needs me to cure
sick slaves
in the barracoons.

After each hurricane season
there are fevers, cholera, smallpox, plague.
Some of the sick can be saved.
Some are lost.
I picture their spirits
flying away.

I sigh, so relieved that I will not
have to travel with slavehunters
and the spies they keep to help them,
the captives who reveal the secret locations
of villages where runaways sneak back and forth,
trading wild guavas for wild yams,
or bananas for boar meat,
spears for vine rope,
or mangos for palm hearts, flower medicines,
herbs. . . .

Lieutenant Death

The weapons of runaways are homemade,
just sharpened branches, not real spears,
and carved wooden guns, which, I have to admit,
from a distance look real!

We catch *cimarrones* with stolen cane knives too,
all three kinds,
the tapered, silver-handled ones used by free men,
with engraved scallop-shell designs,
and the bone-handled, short, leaflike ones,
given to children,
and the fan-shaped, blunt ones,
used by slaves
for cutting sugarcane
to sweeten the chocolate and coffee
of rich men.

Rosa

Secretly, I hide and weep
when I learn that my owner
has agreed to loan me
to the slavehunter,
who brings his hunter-in-training,
his son, the boy with dangerous eyes,
Teniente Muerte,
Lieutenant Death.

Rosa

Spears and stones rain down on us
from high above
as we climb rough stairs
chopped into the wall of a cliff
somewhere out in the wilderness,
in a place I have never seen.

Sharp rocks slice my face and hands.
I will be useless—without healthy fingers,
how can I heal wounds
and fevers?

When the raid is over, many *cimarrones* are dead.
I try to escape, but Lieutenant Death forces me
to watch as he helps his father
collect the ears
of runaways.

Some of the ears come from people
whose names and faces
I know.

Lieutenant Death

I hate to think
what my father would say

if he knew that I am scared
of dogs, both wild and tame,

and ghost stories,
real and imaginary,

and witches,
even the little ones,

and the ears of captives,
still warm. . . .

Rosa

After the raid,
I tend the wounds
of slavehunters
and captives.

Some look at me with fear,
others with hope.

I tend the wounds of a wild dog,
and the slavehunters' huge dogs.
All of them treat me like a nurse,
not a witch.

The grateful dogs make me smile,
even the mean ones, trained to follow the tracks
of barefoot men.

They don't seem to hate
barefoot girls.

Hatred must be
a hard thing to learn.

PART
TWO

The Ten Years' War
1868–78

Rosa

Gathering the green, heart-shaped leaves
of sheltering herbs in a giant forest,

I forget that I am grown now,
with daydreams of my own,

in this place where time
does not seem to exist
in the ordinary way,

and every leaf is a heart-shaped
moment of peace.

Rosa

In the month of October,
when hurricanes loom,
a few plantation owners
burn their fields, and free their slaves,
declaring independence
from Spanish rule.

Slavery all day,
and then, suddenly, by nightfall—freedom!

Can it be true,
as my former owner explains,
with apologies for all the bad years—

Can it be true that freedom only exists
when it is a treasure,
shared by all?

Rosa

Farms and mansions
are burning!

Flames turn to smoke—
the smoke leaps, then fades
and vanishes . . .
making the world
seem invisible.

I am one of the few
free women blessed
with healing skills.

Should I fight with weapons,
or flowers and leaves?

Each choice leads to another—
I stand at a crossroads in my mind,
deciding to serve as a nurse,
armed with fragrant herbs,
fighting a wilderness battle, my own private war
against death.

Rosa

Side by side, former owners and freed slaves
torch the elegant old city of Bayamo.
A song is written by a horseman,
a love song about fighting for freedom
from Spain.
The song is called *"La Bayamesa,"*
for a woman from the burning city of Bayamo,
a place so close to my birthplace, my home. . . .

Soon I am called *La Bayamesa* too,
as if I have somehow been transformed
into music, a melody, the rhythm of words. . . .

I watch the flames, feel the heat,
inhale the scent of torched sugar
and scorched coffee. . . .
I listen to voices,
burning a song in the smoky sky.

The old life is gone, my days are new,
but time is still a mystery
of wishes, and this sad, confusing fragrance.

Rosa

The Spanish Empire refuses to honor
liberty for any slave who was freed by a rebel,
so even though the planters
who used to own us
no longer want to own humans,
slavehunters still roam
the forest, searching, capturing, punishing . . .

so we flee
to the villages
where runaways hide . . .
just like before.

Rosa

In October,
people walk in long chains of strength,
arm in arm, to keep from blowing away.

The wildness of wind, forest, sea
brings storms that move
like serpents,
sweeping trees and cattle
up into the sky.

During hurricanes, even the wealthy
wander like beggars,
seeking shelter,
arm in arm with the poor.

Rosa

War and storms make me feel old,
even though I am still young enough
to fall in love.

I meet a man, José Francisco Varona,
a freed slave,
in the runaway slave village we call Manteca,
because we have plenty of lard to use as cooking oil,
the lard we get
by hunting wild pigs.

We travel through the forest together,
trading lard for the fruit, corn, and yams
grown by freed slaves and runaways,
who live together in other hidden towns
deep in the forest, and in dark caves.

José and I agree to marry.
Together, we will serve as nurses,
healing the wounds of slavery,
and the wounds of war.

Rosa

The forest is a land of natural music—
tree frogs, nightingales, wind,
and the winglets of hummingbirds
no bigger than my thumbnail—
hummingbirds the size of bees
in a forest the size of Eden.

José and I travel together,
walking through mud, thorns,
clouds of wasps, mosquitoes, gnats,
and the mist that hides
graceful palm trees,
and the smoke that hides burning huts,
flaming fields, orchards, villages, forts—
anything left standing by Spain
is soon torched by the rebels.

José carries weapons,
his horn-handled machete,
and an old gun of wood and metal,
moldy and rusted,
our only protection against an ambush.

The Spanish soldiers dress in bright uniforms,
like parakeets.
They march in columns, announcing
their movements
with trumpets and drums.

We move silently, secretly.
We are invisible.

Rosa

A Spanish guard calls, *¡Alto!* Halt!
¿Quién vive? Who lives?
He wants us to stop, but we slip away.

He shouts: *mambí* savages,
and even though *mambí* is not a real word,
we imagine he chooses it
because he thinks it sounds Cuban, Taíno Indian,
or African, or mixed—a word from the language
of an enslaved tribe—
Congo, Arará, Carabalí, Bibí, or Gangá.

Mambí,
we catch the rhythmic word,
and make it our own,
a name for our newly invented warrior tribe
made up of freed slaves fighting side by side
with former owners,
all of us fighting together,
against ownership of Cuba
by the Empire of Spain,
a ruler who refuses
to admit that slaves
can ever be free.

José

Dark wings, a dim moonglow,
the darting of bats,
not the big ones that suck blood
and eat insects,
but tiny ones, butterfly-sized,
the kind of bat
that whisks out of caves to sip nectar
from night-blooming blossoms,
the fragrant white flowers my Rosa calls
Cinderella,
because they last only half a night.

Rosa leads the bats away from our hut.
They follow her light, as she holds up a gourd
filled with fireflies, blinking.

I laugh, because our lives, here in the forest,
feel reversed—
we build a palm-thatched house to use
as a hospital,
but everything wild that belongs outdoors
keeps moving inside,
and our patients, the wounded, feverish
mambí rebels,

who should stay in their hammocks resting—
they keep getting up,
to go outside,
to watch Rosa, with her hands of light,
leading the bats far away.

Lieutenant Death

They think they're free.
I know they're slaves.

I used to work for the Holy Brotherhood
of plantation owners, but now I work
for the Crown of Spain.

Swamps, mountains, jungle, caves . . .
I search without resting, I seek the reward
I will surely collect, just as soon as I kill
the healer they call Rosa *la Bayamesa,*
a witch who cures wild *mambí* rebels
so they can survive
to fight again.

Lieutenant-General Valeriano Weyler y Nicolau, Marquis of Tenerife, Empire of Spain

When the witch is dead,
and the rebels are defeated,
I will rest my sore arms and tired legs
in the healing hot springs on this island of fever
and ghostly, bat-infested caves.

If the slavehunter fails,
I will catch her myself.
I will kill the witch, and keep her ear in a jar,
as proof that owners cannot free their slaves
without Spain's approval

and as proof
that all rebels in Cuba
are doomed.

Rosa

Rumors make me short of breath,
anxious, fearful, desperate.

People call me brave, but the truth is:
Rumors of slavehunters terrify me!

Who could have guessed that after all these years,
the boy I called Lieutenant Death
when we were both children
would still be out here, in the forest,
chasing me, now,
hunting me, haunting me. . . .

Who would have imagined
such stubborn dedication? . . .
If only he would change sides
and become one of us, a stubborn,
determined, weary nurse,
fighting this daily war
against death!

José

Rosa's fame as a healer brings danger.
She cannot leave our hut,
where the patients need her,
so I travel alone to a field of pineapples
where a young Spanish soldier lies wounded
in his bright uniform,
his head resting between mounds
of freshly harvested fruit.

The leaves of the pineapple plants
are gray and sharp, like machetes
the tips of the leaves cut my arms,
but I do my best to treat the boy's wounds.
I do this for Rosa, who wants to heal all.
I do it for Rosa, but the boy-soldier thanks me,
and after I feed him and give him water,
he tells me he wants to change sides.

He says he will be Cuban now, a *mambí* rebel.
He tells me he was just a young boy
who was taken
from his family in Spain,
a child who was put on a ship,

forced to sail to this island, forced to fight.
He tells me he loves Cuba's green hills,
and hopes to stay, survive, be a farmer,
find a place to plant crops. . . .

Together, we agree to try
to heal the wounds between our countries.
I help him take off his uniform.
I give him mine.

Rosa

We experiment
like scientists.

One flower cures
only certain fevers.

We try another.
We fail, then try a root, leaf,
moss, or fern. . . .

One petal fails.
Another succeeds.

José and I are both learning
how to learn.

Lieutenant Death

The witch
can be heard
singing in treetops.

The witch
can be seen—
a shadow
in caves.

I search,
and I search.

She vanishes,
just like the maddening
morning mists
and the wild
mambí rebels.

They attack.
We retreat.
They hide.
We seek.

Rosa

Itchy *guao* leaves,
biting mosquitoes,
and invisible, no-see-um *chinches,*
burrowing ticks, worms, and fungus,
growing in the flesh of the feet.

Gangrene, leprosy, amputations,
I never give myself permission
to look or sound horrified . . .

until I'm alone
at the end of the day,
alone, with the music
of nightingales.

José

We have seventeen patients
in our thatched hut
hidden by forest
and protected by guards,
dogs, traps, and tales of ghosts.

Seventeen feverish, bleeding, burning,
broken men, with bayonet wounds,
and women in childbirth,
and newborn babies . . .

seventeen helpless people,
all depending on us,
seventeen lives, blessings, burdens.

How can we heal them?
We are so weary!
Who will heal us?

Rosa

Grateful families give us chickens,
guinea hens and coconuts,
sweet potatoes,
cornmeal,
a hat, a knife,
a kettle,
a kerchief.

New mothers name their sons José
and their daughters Rosa.
Orphans stay with us,
working alongside the young Spaniard,
who chose to change sides,
and become Cuban.

True healers never charge any money for cures.
The magic hidden inside flowers and trees
is created by the fragrant breath of God—
who are we to claim payment
for miracles?

Who are we to imagine
that the forest belongs to us?

Now, if only God who made the petals
and roots
will grant me one more gift—
a peaceful mind,
escape from the rumors that haunt me,
tales of prowling slavehunters,
warnings about Lieutenant Death.

José

We move all our patients into a cave,
a cathedral of stone,
where Rosa hopes to feel safe.

Crystals glow in the light
of palm-leaf torches
and living fireflies.

The stones seem to move like clouds,
forming bridges, pillars, fountains. . . .

Rosa tells me she feels like one of those statues
that hold up the roofs of old buildings.
I picture the two of us, carved and polished,
motionless, yet alive,
holding up our roof of hope.

Rosa

Hiding in this cave makes me remember
the secret village where runaway slaves
and freed slaves all hid together
during the early months
of this endless war.

The houses were made of reeds and palms,
green houses that looked just like forest.

We built them in a circle,
and at the center, hidden,
we built a church of reeds,
where we would have loved to sing
if we did not always have to be hiding
and silent.

Now, in the cave, I hum quietly.
My voice echoes, and grows.
I sound so much braver and stronger
than I feel.

José

I dream of a farm
with one cow, one horse,
oxen for plowing,
chickens and guinea hens
for Holy Day meals,
and a small grove of trees,
coffee and cacao
shaded by mangos.

I dream of cornfields,
sweet potatoes, bananas,
and a palm-bark house
with a palm-thatch roof,
and a floor of earth,
a porch,
two rocking chairs,
and a view of green wilderness
stretching, like time. . . .

Rosa

Cave of Nightmares,
Cave of Pirates, Cave of Neptune,
Cave of the Generals,
Lagoon of Fish,
Rosa's Cave.

How many names
can one place have?
How many tales
of frightened people hiding,
and blind creatures thriving,
tales of mermaids, sea serpents,
giants, and ghosts. . . .

I leave my handprint on glittering crystal
beside cave paintings made in ancient times—
circles, moons, suns, stars;
my palm, the fingers,
star-shaped too. . . .

Ten years of war.
How many battles
can one island lose?

Lieutenant-General Valeriano Weyler y Nicolau, Marquis of Tenerife, Empire of Spain

We call Cuba our Ever-Faithful Isle,
yet these wild *mambí* rebels are loyal
only to the jungle, and their illusions
of freedom.

We leave the land smoking—
each farm and town turns to ash.

The barracoons where slaves
should be sleeping are empty.

The flames look like scars
on the red, sticky clay
of this maddening island
ruled by mud and mosquitoes.

Rosa

In order to talk to my patients I learn
a few words from each of many languages,
the words of African and native
Cuban Indian tribes,
and all the dialects of the provinces of Spain.

I even invent my own secret codes,
but the ones taught by birds are the best,
especially when mixed
with the music of conch-shell trumpets,
bamboo flutes, rattles, drums,
and the Canary Islanders'
language of Silbo,
a mystery of whistles.

Animals and plants help me learn
how to understand all these ways of knowing
what people are trying to say.
The ears of a horse show anger, or fear.
The eyes of oxen tell of weariness.
Voices of birds chant borders around nests.

Yellow acacia flowers whisper secrets of love.
Green reeds play a wild, windy music.

Pink oleanders are a poisonous message
that warns:
¡Cuidado! Beware!
Fragrant blue rosemary speaks of memory.
White poppies mean sleep.
White yarrow foretells war.

José

The most famous of our *mambí* generals
are called the Fox and the Lion.
Máximo Gómez is the Fox, slender and pale,
a foreigner from the island of Hispaniola.
First he was a Spanish soldier,
then a rebel,
and now we think of him as Cuban.

The Lion is Antonio Maceo, our friend since birth,
a local man of mixed race.
Some call him the Bronze Titan,
because he is powerful, and calm.

The Fox loves to quote philosophers, poets,
and the Proverbs of King Solomon.
He tells Rosa that those who save lives are wise,
like trees that bear life-giving fruit.

The Lion adds that kindness to animals
and children
is a part of Rosa's natural gift,
but healing the wounds of enemy soldiers
is a strange mercy that floats down
from heaven.

Rosa

The Lion and the Fox
visit our hospital huts and caves.
We have many now.
We travel from one to another,
carrying medicines, and hope.

I wear an ammunition belt,
and an old gun, a carbine,
to make José happy, because he insists
that I must learn to defend myself
against spies.

Lieutenant Death

I watch
from a treetop,
looking down
at the top
of her head.

So simple.
Her hair
in a kerchief.
Her gun,
rusty, useless . . .

She is not
what I expected
of someone so famous
for miracles.

I take aim,
then wait,
searching. . . .
How did she do it. . . ?
Is she a real witch. . . ?
How does she make herself
vanish?

Rosa

A man is carried into the hospital, wounded—
he fell from a tree.

I know his face, and I can tell that he
recognizes me.
We were children, we were enemies . . .
Now he is my patient,
but why should I cure him,
wasting precious medicines
on a spy who must have been sent
to kill me?

Each choice leads to another.
I am a nurse.
I must heal the wounded.
How well the Lion knows me! Didn't he say
that curing the enemies
is not my own skill, but a mercy from God?

Each choice leads to another.
I am a nurse.
I must heal.

Lieutenant Death

I sneak away,
my arm splinted,
my head bandaged.
Now I know
where Rosa *la Bayamesa,*
the cave nurse from Bayamo,
hides her patients—
in a hospital
of secrets,
surrounded by jungle,
walls of tree trunks,
fences of thorns—
now I know,
and I can sell
this information
for many smooth
round coins
of gold!

Rosa

The parakeet-bright Spanish soldiers
come marching
with torches, and Mausers, and trumpets.

We are forced to escape, move our patients, hide,
find a new home, new hope, a new cave . . .
although clearly, this one too is ancient—
every wall and spire of crystal
bears the marks of other fugitives,
people who hid here
long ago—
people who left
their handprints on stone.

Will I ever feel safe?
Can I continue?
When will I rest,
if my sleep
always turns
into whirlwinds,
this spiral
of nightmares? . . .

José

One more escape.
We are safe.
We whisper.
We hide.
We hope.
We explore
our new home,
this vast, glittering cavern
of crystals, darkness, silence. . . .

Rosa

The caves, this stench, the bat dung, urine,
frogs, fish, lizards, *majá* snakes,
all so pale and ghostly, some eyeless, all blind . . .

and the crystals, these archways and statues,
these flowers of stone . . .

shadows, pottery, bones . . .
the skeletons of those who hid here
so long ago, when I was a child,
when I was a slave . . .

Rosa

We send messages to the Fox and the Lion.
No one else knows whcre we are.

We learn to live in darkness,
without so many lanterns and torches,
fireflies, and candles
made from the wax
of wild bees.

We drink wild honey
instead of sugarcane syrup.

We are far from any farms or towns.
We eat the blind lizards and ghost-fish.

We know how to live
with the stench of black vomit,
yellow fever in its final stage. . . .

Rosa

The fevers and wounds of war are deadly,
yet somehow
many of our patients survive to go back out,
and fight again.

Our former owners have been healed here.
They treat us like brothers and sisters, not slaves.

The Fox and the Lion keep our location secret.
We are not found on their maps,
or in their diaries.

Everyone here knows the truth—
I am a nurse, not a sorceress.

I am just a woman of weary, wild hopes—
not a magician, not a witch.

José

Rosa remembers the names
of all who pass through her hands,

the patients who survive, and those who rise,
breath vanishing into the sky. . . .

It's all she can offer,
just forest medicines,

and her memory, reciting the names of people
along with the names of the flowers.

Rosa

Ten years of war are over.
A treaty. Peace.
So many lives were lost.
Was anything gained?
The Spanish Empire still owns
this suffering island,
and most of the planters
still own slaves.

Only a few of us were set free
by rebels who have been defeated.
Spanish law still calls me a slave.
Lieutenant Death has not lost
his power.

PART
Three

The Little War
1878–80

Rosa

Too soon,
the battles
begin again.

Mercifully,
this new war
is brief.

Tragically,
this new war
is futile.

Sometimes, war feels
like just one more
form of slavery.

José

We heal the wounded
just like before.

We hide in the jungle
just like before.

We are older.
Are we wiser?

Sometimes war feels
like a lonely child's game,
one that explodes
out of control.

Rosa

Between wars,
José and I were just
a man and his wife.
We were free
to stay together.
José never had to leave me
to scout, or hunt,
or fight.

Between wars,
life was heavenly,
except when the slavehunters
were near,
with our names
on a list.

José

Mothers come to us
with tales of children
lost in the chaos.

They must imagine
that we know how to find
little ones who hide in barns,
and teenagers armed with anger.

If we knew how to find
the lost, we would know
how to rediscover
the parts of our minds
left behind
in battle.

Rosa

This is how you heal a wound:
Clean the flesh.
Sew the skin.
Pray for the soul.
Wait.

José

A wounded child tells me
he has never seen a grown man
who was proud to be a nurse.

Women's work, he mocks,
but I smile—what could be
more manly than knowing
the strange names and magical uses
of sturdy medicinal trees
with powerful,
hidden roots?

Lieutenant Death

I feel old,
but I am young enough
and strong enough
to know that one battle
leads to another.

As this Little War ends,
I ask myself
how many years will pass
before I finally have my chance
to kill Rosa the Witch,
and her husband, José,
and the rebels they heal,
year after year,
like legends kept alive
with nothing more magical
than words?

Rosa

The Little War?
How can there be
a little war?

Are some deaths
smaller than others,
leaving mothers
who weep
a little less?

José is hopeful that soon
there will be another chance
to gain independence from Spain,
and freedom for slaves,

but all I see is death, always the same,
always enormous, never little,
no matter how many women come to help me,
asking to be trained in the art of learning
the names of forest flowers
and the names of brave people.

PART
Four

The War of Independence
1895–98

Rosa

This new war begins with rhymes,
the *Simple Verses* of Martí,
Cuba's most beloved poet.
José Martí,
who leads with words
not just swords.

He is the one who inspires
the Fox and the Lion to fight again,
even though Martí was just a child-poet
during the other wars,
a teenager arrested
for writing about Cuba's longing
for independence from Spain
and freedom from slavery.

Martí is the son of a Spaniard.
He writes of love for his Spanish father,
and he writes of the need for peace—
yet he fights.
He tells me the forest comforts him
more deeply than the musical waves
of the most beautiful beach.

Martí soon loses his life
in battle.

I cannot save the poet
from bullets.

José

Once again, the Fox and the Lion gallop
across our green mountains and farms,
burning the sugar fields and coffee groves,
the tobacco plantations, scented smoke rising
like a wild storm
of hope. . . .

Once again, I guard Rosa's hospitals
while she nurses the sick and wounded
in secret places, thatched huts,
and glittering caves. . . .

Once again, we travel invisibly,
slipping through lines of Spanish forts and troops
on moonless nights,
puffing cigars to make our movements
look like the blinking dance
of fireflies. . . .

Lieutenant Death

Once again, light men and dark
fight side by side,
as if there had never been slavery. . . .
I shake my head, still unable to believe
that slavery ended in 1886—
all the skills of my long life,
all the arts of slavehunting
will be lost. . . .

At least I do not feel useless—
there are still indentured Canary Islanders,
white slaves, citizens of Spain.
When they run, I chase them, just like before—
just like the old days,
when there were Africans of every tribe,
and the indentured Chinese, and the Irish,
and Mayan Indians from Yucatán. . . .

Nothing makes sense now.
I long to retire, on a farm with a view
of the sunset,
and a porch with a rocking chair . . .
just as soon as I kill
the old witch. . . .

Captain-General Valeriano Weyler y Nicolau, Marquis of Tenerife, Empire of Spain

This new rebellion must end swiftly—
I have promised victory
within thirty days.

I will send out a proclamation
ordering all peasants to report immediately
to cities where they cannot grow crops
for feeding rebels,
their cousins,
their brothers. . . .

I will give the peasants eight days
to reach them,
these *campamentos de reconcentración,*
a name of my own invention—
reconcentration camps,
a brilliant new concept,
the only strategy that can ensure
absolute control of all the land
while being portrayed
as a way of keeping peasants guarded
for their own safety.

When eight days have passed,
any man, woman, or child
found in the countryside
will be shot.

Rosa

Eight days?
Eight days.
Weyler is a madman.
How can he expect
so many to travel so far
so quickly?

Eight days.
Impossible.
Thousands of families
will not even hear
about the order
to reconcentrate
in camps
within eight days.

Silvia

I am eleven years old, and my life is this farm.
My father is dead,
and my mother is sick.
My life is planting, harvesting,
and caring for my twin brothers.

Only eight days . . .
impossible to believe.

I do not pack our things right away.
First I wait to see if this strange rumor
is true.
Then, brightly uniformed troops
burn our house,
swooping across our farm like hungry birds,
stealing the wagon and oxen, horses, mules,
even the chickens,
and the cow we need
for milk to feed the twins,
my baby brothers—
will they starve?

Nothing is left to pack, not even clothes,
so I walk away from the farm,

leading my mother,
and carrying the babies,
while my eyes watch the mountains,
and my thoughts turn
toward tales of healers
the legend of Rosa. . . .

Silvia

Long ago, my grandma
was one of Rosa's patients
in a hospital cave—
all my life, I've heard wonderful
tales of healing.

When this new war started,
my grandma told me
how to flee to the caves.

Finding Rosa now seems as likely
as convincing her that I am old enough
to help treat the wounded
by learning the art of mending bones,
using nothing more magical
than the flowers
of jungle trees.

At least I know the names of the flowers—
that much, my grandma taught me.

Rosa

I climb a palm tree
and watch the madness
from my hidden perch.

Soldiers herd peasants
into a camp, fenced and guarded,
surrounded by trenches and forts.

I see no houses or tents, no hospital. . . .
All I can do is watch with silent tears
as wounded men, pregnant women,
and helpless children are herded
into the camp—
just another name
for prison.

Silvia

My mother is weak,
so I have to be strong.

Obediently, I shuffle into the Spanish Army's
strange camp, this reconcentration camp
where I do not know what to expect.
I clutch my little brothers tightly
in my arms,
secretly wondering if the armed guards can tell
that I am thinking of Rosa's miraculous flowers
in caves of crystal,
deep caverns
of hidden peace.

Rosa

When night falls,
I climb down from the palm tree
and slip away, back to the forest,
wishing I could take them all with me,
all the refugees flocking like birds
lost in a storm, flying to the mountains
to find trees that look like sturdy guardians
with leafy branches that whisper
soft lullabies of comfort.

A few refugees find us.
Some are the children
of women who helped me
nurse the wounded
long ago. . . .

I teach the granddaughters
of women whose lives I saved
and men whose lives were lost.

José

We try to help the refugees
who find us.
Rosa entertains frightened children,
pretending to be a magical dentist,
as she reaches into the mouth of a man
whose throbbing tooth must come out
if he is going to survive.

She seems to be pulling the tooth
with her bare fingers.
I am the only one who knows
that she hides a tiny key
in her hand, a simple tool
to ease the man's suffering.

When the tooth is out,
he whispers thanks,
and he tries to laugh a little bit,
making his pain seem to vanish,
a comfort to the startled,
giggling children.

I am the only one
who sees Rosa's sorrow,

the only one who knows
how hard it is to start again,
another war of fever and wounds,
the exhaustion created
by endless hope . . .

Silvia

Hunger, fever,
my mother's moans,
my brothers' shrieks,
the madness, cruelty, or kindness
from each new neighbor,
all these weeping strangers
huddled into makeshift houses
of leaf and twig, palm frond and mud.
Patience, impatience, hopelessness, hope . . .

I stare at the forts
with holes in the wood
that look like eyes—
holes for the guns
of soldiers
who watch us
day and night.

Rosa

The numbers are impossible.
I cannot heal so many.

Women come as volunteers.
I teach them simple cures.

Garlic for parasites, indigo for lice,
wild ginger to soothe a cough,
jasmine for calming jittery nerves,
guava to settle the stomach,
aloe for burns.

Is there at least one wild,
fragrant remedy
for healing sorrow
and curing fear?

Silvia

Beyond the fence there is a special tree
for hanging those who try
to escape.

Corridors of shacks built from mud and sticks,
babies too weak to eat or cry,
yellow fever, cholera, smallpox, tetanus,
malaria, dysentery, starvation,
my mother's feverish, distant eyes . . .

this camp is the ash and soot
of human shame.

José

Rage, fury, no time for fear,
no room for sadness.

We like to joke
about Spanish soldiers owning
only the small, foot-shaped parts of Cuba
beneath their own feet.

We like to say that we have learned
how to appear to obey the Spanish Empire's laws
without actually obeying.

Our lives are caves
filled with secrets.

Silvia

Today I am twelve.
My mother is in heaven.
I feel twelve thousand.

An oxcart took her.
The driver is dark, with a kind smile.
I ask him why he does this work,
and he explains that he is a volunteer
from the Brothers of Charity and Faith,
a church group of black men who tend the sick
and bury the dead, even executed criminals
abandoned by their own families.

I ask him if he knows
how I can find Rosa *la Bayamesa,*
the Cave Nurse of Cuba.

He looks surprised, but he answers quietly:
First you will have to cross the fence—
first you will have to escape.

Silvia

The oxcart comes every afternoon,
People call it the death-cart.
But I think of it as a chariot
driven by my friend, an angel,
a Brother of Charity and Faith.

The angel-man brings me
tiny bits of smuggled food,
but there is never enough,
and my brothers are turning
into shadows.

I feed them
imaginary meals
of air.

Rosa

The wind
is an evil wind.

I make rope from strips of hibiscus wood,
and splints of palm bark,
my only hope for mending bones.

My greatest fear is of being useless,
so I pierce and drain infected wounds
with the thorns of bitter orange trees,
and I treat the sores of smallpox
with the juice of boiled yams.

I use the perfumed leaves
of bay rum trees
to mask the scent
of death.

José

General Máximo Gómez, the Fox,
asks Rosa to choose twelve trustworthy men
who can help us build a bigger hospital,
so sturdy and so well-hidden
that it will never be found
or attacked.

My wife says two trustworthy men
will be enough.

She tells the Fox that she is strong.
She wants to help chop the wood
for building our new home.

Silvia

Concentrate. Reconcentrate.
Mass, cluster, bunch, and heap.
Weyler's camp makes my arms and legs
so skinny that even my mind feels hungry.
Concentrate. Reconcentrate.
Plan, pay attention, focus, think.
I am alone now. My brothers
are with my mother.
The oxcart comes and goes.

The Brother of Charity and Faith
sees my hopelessness.
He lets me ride with him,
hiding in the oxcart.
I am leaving.
Where will I go?

Silvia

The wagon creaks,
wheels sing . . .
the night is moonless,
my body feels ancient,
my mind feels new.

The driver turns and smiles.
He hands me his cigar, a blinking light.
He shows me how to pretend
that I am a firefly.

He points to a hole in the fence,
puts his finger to his lips,
then draws a map in the sky—
a picture of the way
to find Rosa.

Silvia

I dance through the hole in my fenced life,
moving the make-believe firefly with my hand,
not my mouth, because I am afraid I would not
be able to stop coughing.

The tiny light rises, dips, flits,
just a foul-scented cigar
pretending to fly,
but it carries a memory
of the oxcart driver's hand,
showing me how to find the woman
who once saved my grandma's life.

Rosa's cave is the only place I long to be
now that my family is in heaven.

Silvia

Tree frogs, screech owls, the dancing leaves
of feathery ferns, the fragrant petals
of wild orchids.

Night wings, crickets,
imagining secrets,
wondering which flowers
might save a life,
and which could be dangerous,
if I don't learn quickly, if I feed a patient
just a little too much . . .

Will Rosa teach me?
Is Rosa real, or just one more
of those comforting tales
the old folks tell
at bedtime?

Silvia

Moonless thunder, silent lightning, the tracks
of mountain ponies.

Mambí birdcalls, a stream, tall reeds, the song
of a waterfall, my own tumbling, exhausted,
singing wild hopes.

A trail, more hoofprints, a woman in blue
with long, loose black hair just like my own.

The whistle of a Canary Islander,
speaking the secret language of Silbo.

My bare, bony feet running, following,
racing toward Rosa. . . .

José

All night I stand guard, singing silently
inside my mind, to keep myself awake.

In daylight I sleep, while others watch.
A whistle reaches into my dream . . .

the face of a pale, skeletal child,
two eyes, deep green pools
of fear. . . .

Silvia

Does the old man in the forest
know that he sings in his sleep?

I stare, he stares,
then we both smile.
Rosa, I hear myself chant the name
over and over,
begging for a flower-woman
who will teach me how to save lives.

I tell the old man that I already know
the names of the blossoms, all I need is a chance
to learn their magic.

With a sigh, he says,
Yes of course, one more child
is always welcome,
follow me. . . .

Rosa

The new girl is so thin and pale
that I cannot let her help me
until she has learned
how to heal herself.

I make her eat, sleep, rest.
She resists.

I see a story in her eyes.
She thinks she has no right to eat
while so many others starve.

Silvia

Rosa is a bully.
I thought she would be sweet and kind,
but she forces me to sip my soup,
and she stitches a cut on my forehead,
just a scratch from a thorn in the forest,
but she studies it the way I studied the forts
at the camp, with the holes for guns
that look like eyes.

The needle hurts, the thread itches.
Maybe I don't want to be a nurse after all.
Speed, Rosa tells me, is the best painkiller,
so she stitches my skin quickly, calmly,
her expression as mysterious as a book
written in some foreign alphabet
from a faraway land.

She looks at my tongue,
puts her finger on my wrist,
explains that she is counting my pulse.
She tells me I do not have leprosy or plague,
measles, tetanus, scarlet fever,
jaundice, or diptheria.

By now, she adds, you must be immune
to yellow fever,
and malaria, well, that is an illness most Cubans
will carry around
all our lives.

I picture myself lugging a suitcase loaded
with heavy diseases. . . .
I daydream a ship, an escape route, the ocean. . . .

Rosa

The girl is well enough to learn.
I show her one cure at a time.
A poultice of okra for swelling.
Arrowroot to draw poison out of a wound.
Cactus fruit for soothing a cough.
Hibiscus juice for thirst.
Honey for healing.

I show her the workshop where saddles are made
with leather tanned by pomegranate juice,
and I show her the workshop
where hats are woven
from the dry, supple fiber of palm fronds,
and the place where candles
of beeswax are shaped
to light the rare books
from which cave children learn
how to read comforting Psalms,
and the *Simple Verses* of José Martí,
our poet of memory,
our memory of hope. . . .

Rosa

Young people are like the wood of a balsa tree,
light and airy—they can float, like rafts,
like boats. . . .

José and I are the rock-hard wood
of a *guayacán* tree,
the one shipbuilders call Tree of Life
because it is so dense
and heavy with resin
that it sinks,
making the best propeller shafts—
the wood will never rot,
but it cannot float. . . .

Young people drift on airy daydreams.
Old folks help hold them in place.

Silvia

Rosa helps me see the caves
in her own way.
I gaze around at the forest,
where she has been free,
so alive in this wonder,
where trees grow like castle towers,
with windows opening
onto rooms of sunlight.

I can no longer imagine
living anywhere else,
without this garden of orchids
and bright macaws.

I think of all I know
about tales of castles.
There is always a dungeon,
and a chapel,
bells of hope. . . .

Rosa

Silvia tells me that she used to visit
her grandparents in town.

They kept caged birds,
and in the evenings they walked,
carrying the cages up a hill
to watch the sunset.
Inside each cage, the captive birds
sang and fluttered, wings dancing.

Silvia admits that she always wondered
whether the birds imagined they were flying,
or maybe they understood the limitations
of bamboo bars, the walls of each tiny cage.

Now I ask myself about my own limitations,
trying to serve as mother and grandmother
to a child who has lost
everyone she ever loved.

Rosa

The Fox has named me
the first woman Captain
of Military Health,
the first Cuban rebel army nurse
who will be remembered
by name.

I think of all the others
who went before me
in all three wars,
curing the wounded, healing the sick,
nameless women, forgotten now,
their voices and hands
just part of the forest,
whispering like pale *yagruma* leaves
in a breeze.

On hot days, even the shade
from a *yagruma* leaf
offers soothing medicine,
the magic of one quiet moment
of peace.

José

Warnings fly from every direction.
Lieutenant Death, the old slavehunter,
never gives up.
He is seen far too often, tracking, stalking,
hunting his prey.

The price for Rosa's ear grows—
her ear, the proof of her death.

I climb a towering palm tree,
to watch the movements of shadows below.
I wait, studying the shapes to see
which might be wounded rebels,
coming to Rosa for help,
and which could be Death,
bringing his nickname,
even though Rosa healed his flesh
so long ago.

She did not know
how to heal
his soul.

Lieutenant Death

Strangler fig, candle tree, dragon's blood.
The names of forest plants lead me
toward Rosa the Witch.

I can never let anyone learn my real name,
or there will be rebel vengeance, after I kill her.

She is a madwoman—just yesterday, I heard
that she cleaned and bandaged the wounds
of forty Spanish soldiers,
and that Gómez the Fox let them all go,
seizing only their horses, saddles, and weapons,
leaving them enough food to survive.

No wonder so many young Spanish boys
are switching sides, joining the rebels,
becoming Cubans.

She must be stopped.
It makes no sense, healing her enemies
so they will turn into friends.

Rosa

When I travel
between two hospitals,
I listen to trees that speak
with the movement of leaves.

The horse I ride
sings to me
by twitching his ears,
telling me how much
he hates
the flames of war.

I stroke his mane
to let him know
that I will keep him safe.
I hope it is true. . . .

Lieutenant Death

I camp beneath
a shelf of rock,
almost a cave,
I must be close. . . .

I crush a flower bud,
popping it
to squirt the juice
that would have turned
into a blossom
with nectar
for honeybees.

Silvia

How long have Rosa and I roamed
these green, musical hills?

Each step my little mountain pony takes
has a rhythm, the music of movement,
a way to make the most of every chance
to heal a wound, cure a fever, save a life. . . .

We ride through dark night,
surrounded by the beauty of owl songs,
tree frogs, cicada melodies,
the whoosh of bat wings
and leaves in a breeze,
all of it teaching me
how to sing without being discovered
by soldiers who would find us and kill us
if my song turned into words. . . .

Rosa

The scars of fear burn so intensely
that I no longer ride my horse
with a metal bit in his soft, sensitive mouth.

I do not use a bridle of rope
or a saddle of leather
or spurs of sharp metal.
I've learned how to guide the smooth gait
of my Paso Fino mountain horse
by shifting my weight and my gaze
ever so slightly,
just enough to tell him
where I want to go.

I've learned how to choose a direction
with my knees, and my hands,
and my hopes. . . .

Lieutenant Death

I wear a red tassel on my hat
to protect me against Rosa's evil eye.

The caves are endless.
If I never find Rosa,
will the cave serpents
find me?

Breathless, I race
back out, into sunlight,
where small blue lizards
and huge green iguanas
bob their heads
as if they are mocking me
with wicked, silent laughter. . . .

Has the witch cursed me?
Am I mad to think of such things
when I should be hunting, tracking,
hard at work?

Silvia

Before the war, a funeral meant bells,
trumpets, drums,
white flowers, and black horses
wearing black tassels.

Now we just kneel, then rise to our feet,
wondering why there are no priests
out here in the forest . . .
no tombstones or gravediggers with shovels,
just children with machetes tied to poles
for digging, and hardly any weeping
or singing, or flowers. . . .

I wonder what the king of Spain
would think if he could see us.
He's just a boy, around my age.
I've seen his picture, with sad eyes
and no smile—does he understand anything
about this war?

Lieutenant Death

I march beside an army of land crabs,
their orange claws clacking like drums.
Crocodiles leap from the swamps,
while tree rats stare down at them, haunted.

Green parrots swoop
above the swollen trunks
of potbellied palm trees.

Vultures nest in tunnels of mud.
A hummingbird hovers beside my ear.
Pink flamingos flock past me, cackling.
At night, a bat sips nectar
from white flowers
the size of my fist.

Fever seizes my mind.
Panic, anger, then fear again . . .
So many years in this jungle,
and now, here I am,
alone . . . lost . . . alone. . . .

José

We no longer have enough food
for so many patients.

Silvia and I go out to gather
wild yams and honey.

The child tells me her grandmother
showed her how to cure sadness
by sucking the juice of an orange,
while standing on a beach.

Toss the peels onto a wave.
Watch the sadness float away.

Rosa

One night, a hole appears in the thatch
of our biggest hospital's roof.

A woman's face.
A child.

The boy descends
as if floating.

He is sick. Heal him,
his mother pleads.

I look around, and realize
that she came through the roof
because the door was too crowded
with families weeping, rebels moaning,
women begging. . . .

This war is a serpent,
growing, stretching. . . .

Silvia

In wild swamps,
I clean and bandage
the gunshot wounds
of Spanish soldiers.

The youngest are children,
boys of eleven, twelve, thirteen. . . .

Those who survive thank me
with words and smiles,
even when the only medicines I have
are bits of lemon juice and ash.

Silvia

Sometimes we are so hungry
that we sing about making an *ajiaco* stew,
the kind where a kettle is filled with all sorts
of meats and vegetables.

It takes many cooks to make an *ajiaco*.
Each person brings only one slice of meat
or one potato, one *malanga* tuber or onion,
or salt from the sea.

When the stew is ready, everyone dances.
At the beach, kickfighting swimmers show off
the methods they've learned
for battling sharks.

Even though my *ajiaco* is an imaginary one,
I end up feeling that
something special has happened.
I fall asleep dreaming of music and friends,
not food.
I fall asleep with my whole family
all around me, still alive. . . .

Captain-General Valeriano Weyler y Nicolau, Marquis of Tenerife, Empire of Spain

In a palace in Havana,
I practice the art of the lance game,
riding a wooden horse around and around
on a carousel pushed by a slave.

Each time I complete the circle,
I stab my narrow sword
through a wooden ring.

When this war is over
and I have won,
I will buy one of those fancy
new mechanical carousels
with many painted horses
and a golden ring.

Silvia

Today the most amazing thing happened!
A man came from far away, to present the Fox
with a jeweled ceremonial sword
made by Tiffany,
someone very famous in New York,
the city where this visitor works
for a newspaper called the *Journal*,
a foreign name I can never
hope to pronounce.

When I asked Rosa why a newspaper
would care so much about our island,
I found her answer troubling.

She said tales of suffering sell newspapers
that make readers feel safe,
because they are so far away
from the horror. . . .

Silvia

More and more young people come to join us.
El Grillo, the Cricket, is small, dark, and lively.
His nickname is earned by chattering.
He is only eleven, but his job is important.
He helps the Spanish deserter
who cooks for the Fox.
How odd it must feel to work as a kitchen boy
in this forest, without a real kitchen,
especially on days when there is no food.

Some of the officers are only fourteen.
The Flag Captain is a girl my age.
When Spanish soldiers see her, they hesitate.
They are not accustomed
to shooting girls.

The Sisters of Shade weave hats
to bring relief from the sun.
They show me how to sew
a padded amulet of cloth
to wear over my heart, as protection
against bullets.

José

Each rebel has a nickname.
El Indio Bravo wears his black hair long,
like his native Taíno Indian ancestors.
Los Inglesitos have light hair,
so we call them the Englishmen,
even though they speak only Spanish.
Los Pacíficos are the Peaceful Ones.
They grow crops to feed their little ones,
instead of choosing sides in the war.

Nicknames of all sorts are worn proudly,
except for *majá*, which means cave boa,
like the snake that hides in darkness,
waiting for bats—
majá is the name we call cowards
who choose to ride the slowest horses
into battle, so they can be the first
to turn back, and survive
if a retreat is called.

José

War is like the game
of *gallina ciega,* blind hen.
We hide. They seek.
One shot from my old carbine,
and Spanish troops return fire
with thousands of Mauser balls,
cannons, explosives. . . .

So I hide, shoot, and wait
for them to waste ammunition,
firing back at me,
into the forest,
hitting nothing but trees.

Silvia

The wounded are sacred.
We never leave them.
When everyone else
flees the battlefield,
nurses are the ones
who rush to carry
the wounded
to Rosa.

I am learning
how to stay
far too busy
for worries
about dying.

Rosa

Today the children saved us,
our patients, the nurses, my husband, my life.
Spanish soldiers came marching
to the music of trumpets and drums.
Silvia, Cricket, and the Sisters of Shade
ran and grabbed beehives.

I was so weary, I was dreaming.
I had no idea that we were in danger.
I slept through the drumming and buzzing,
cries of fear, shouts of surprise. . . .
Our hives fooled the troops
into fleeing—they do not know
that these bees are stingless.

Now, we feast on wild honey.
We light a candle, and take turns reading
the *Simple Verses* of José Martí.
My favorite is the one about knowing
the strange names of flowers.

José

How strange and sudden
are changes in wartime.

Soon after the victory of beehives,
we suffer a dreadful defeat.
A spy has betrayed the Lion,
revealing his position.
He was ambushed.
He is gone.

The Fox is alone now, only one leader . . .
so many dreams.

Silvia

Our Lion is dead,
but Weyler the Butcher
has been sent back to Spain,
humiliated by his failure
to defeat *mambí* rebels. . . .
How can I decide
whether to weep for the Lion
or celebrate an end to Cuba's
reconcentration?

The camp where my family starved,
and shivered with fever—
the camp is open now—
the guards are gone.

Survivors can leave
if they have
the strength.

PART Five

The Surrender Tree
1898–99

Rosa

No one understands
why a U.S. battleship
has been anchored
in Havana Harbor.

We do not know
how the ship explodes,
killing hundreds of American sailors,
who must have felt so safe
aboard their sturdy warship.

Who can be blamed
for the bomb?

José

After the U.S. battleship *Maine*
explodes in Havana Harbor,
Spain's soldiers in Cuba
are no longer paid or fed
by their own country's
troubled army.

Deserters flee into the mountains
by the hundreds, then by thousands,
coming to us for mercy,
begging to switch sides
and become *mambí* rebels
because we know how to find
roots and wildflowers
to keep ourselves alive.

How swiftly old enemies
turn into friends.

Silvia

Foreign newspaper reporters
flood our valleys and mountains,
journeying to Cuba
from distant places
with strange names.
Some come with cameras,
others with sketchbooks.

Rosa poses calmly.
I smile.
Cricket laughs,
because even though some of the artists
are amazing,
others are sneaky—
one reporter sketches the fat cook,
making him look thin and handsome,
to flatter him
before begging for extra food.

Only José refuses to be photographed
or sketched—he claims he once
knew a man
who posed, and was harmed by the camera,
and has never been the same.

I do not believe that José is afraid.
He just wants to keep our faces
and our hospitals
safely hidden.

Rosa

The countryside is a ghostland
of burned farms and the ashes of houses,
skeletal trees blackened by smoke.

Rumors blossom
and wither like orchids.

Some say the U.S. Cavalry
is here to help us.
Others insist that the Americans
must have bombed
their own warship
just to have an excuse
for fighting in Cuba
so close to the end
of our three wars
for independence.

Silvia

The U.S. Cavalrymen
call themselves Rough Riders
but José calls them Weary Walkers
because fever makes them so weak
that they have to dismount
and lead their horses
through Cuba's swamps.

Some of the northerners
who come to our hospitals with fever
are dark men who laugh
when they call themselves
the Immunes.

They say they were promised
that if they volunteered to fight in Cuba
they would remain healthy—
apparently, in northern lands,
dark people were thought to be safe
from tropical fevers
until Cuba started teaching
northern doctors
the truth.

Rosa

I smile as Silvia tries to learn English
from our new patients, some light, some dark,
all speaking the same odd, birdlike language.

I can't understand
why dark northern soldiers
and light ones
are separated
into different brigades.
The dead are all buried together
in hasty mass graves,
bones touching.

José

I serve as a guide for the Rough Riders,
some of them Cherokee and Chippewa,
others old bear hunters and gold miners,
cattlemen, gamblers, college students,
and doctors.

Rosa will not allow the foreign doctors
to leech blood from feverish men
who are already weak,
or to cover their wounds with a paste
of poisonous mercury and chlorine,
so most of the Rough Riders
are taken away
to their own hospital ships,
where they can be treated
without the help
of my stubborn wife,
even though
she is right. . . .

Rosa

Gómez is truly a clever Fox.
He writes in his diary,
keeping track of every battle,
every movement, every Cuban guide
hired to help the Americans
find their way in our jungle,
as they chase bands of desperate
Spanish soldiers.

I am pleased to see the Fox
writing columns of numbers.
He records each debt, no matter how small.
He promises that every *Pacífico,*
every Peaceful One,
every hardworking farmer will be paid
for each grain of corn, each pig, each hen.

I thank God that some peasants
did not move to the camps.
We survive with food raised
by those who stayed hidden
in remote valleys,
planting by the moon,
and harvesting in sunlight.

Silvia

I watch as foreign soldiers
write letters home
to their families.

Cricket is fascinated too—
he has never been to school.
He can barely write.

One of the Rough Riders tells us
that he is writing to his wife
about us,
and about Rosa,
the way she treats everyone the same,
without taking payment,
or choosing favorites.

Rosa

I travel down to the remnants of camps,
where skeletal people now come and go freely,
walking like ghosts, wandering, grieving.

American nurses hand out food
to those who line up early,
while there is enough.
The nurses wear white-winged hats, like angels.
I meet Clara Barton, with her angel-wing hat.
The famous Red Cross nurse
tells me she is sorry she could not help sooner,
when there was no food
in the camps, and no medicine.
Now she can help,
but for so many, help comes too late.

She gives me a hat
with white wings, a blood-red cross,
the colors of jasmine
and roses.

Silvia

Some of the U.S. Army nurses
are young Lakota Sioux nuns
who have come here to help us
even though their own tribe in the north
has suffered so much, for so long,
starving and dying
in their own distant wars.

One of the nuns
is called Josefina Two Bears.
She promises to take care
of all the orphans
from the camps.

Rosa

In the caves, our pillows were stones
and our beds were moss.

Water trickled from crystal ceilings
with a sound like quiet music.

It was easy to imagine
a peaceful future,
a peaceful past. . . .

Now I sleep in a real bed, dreaming
that I am seated on a green, sunny roadside,
selling flowers—cup-of-gold vine, orange trumpet,
coral vine, flame tree, ghost orchid, roses. . . .

I dream that I am able to sell all these flowers
because it is peacetime,
and blossoms are treasured
for beauty and fragrance,
not potions, not cures. . . .

José

How will I deliver such strange news
to my wife, who has labored so hard
for so long, that even her sleep is not sleep,
but just dreams. . . .

How can I tell her that suddenly
this third war has ended?

If only I could tell her
that we won.

Instead, I must whisper a truth
that seems impossible—
Spain has been defeated,
but Cuba is not victorious.

The Americans have seized power.
Once again, we are the subjects
of a foreign tyrant.

Rosa

We helped them win
their strange victory
against Spain.

We imagined they were here
to help us gain the freedom
we've craved for so long.

We were inspired by their wars
for freedom from England
and freedom for slaves.

We helped them win
this strange victory
over us.

José

They choose a majestic tree,
a *ceiba*, the kapok tree
revered by Cubans,
a sturdy tree with powerful roots.

They choose the shade of spreading branches.
We have to watch from far away.
Even General Gómez,
after thirty years of leading our rebels,
even he is not invited
to the ceremonial surrender.

Spain cedes power before our eyes.
We can only watch from far away
as the Spanish flag is lowered
and the American flag glides upward.

Our Cuban flag
is still forbidden.

Rosa

Silvia has decided
to help the Sioux nuns
build an orphanage
for children
from the camps.

José and I must continue
doing what we can
to heal the wounded
and cure the sick.

Peace will not be paradise,
but at least we can hope
that children like Silvia
and the other orphans
will have their chance
to dream
of new ways
to feel free. . . .

Silvia

I feel like a child again.
I don't know how to behave.

The war is over—
should I dance,
am I free to sing out loud,
free to grow up,
fall in love?

I am free to smile
while the orphans sleep.

I admit that I feel impatient,
so eager to write in a journal,
like the Fox,
writing a record
of all that I have seen. . . .

Peace is not the paradise
I imagined, but it is a chance
to dream. . . .

Author's Note

My grandmother used to speak of a time when her parents had to leave their farm in central Cuba and "go to another place." I had no idea what she meant, until I grew up and read historical accounts of Weyler's reconcentration camps.

My grandmother was born on a farm in central Cuba in 1902. She described Cuba's countryside as so barren from the destruction of war that once, when her whole family was hungry, her father rode off into the wilderness and came back with a river turtle. That one turtle was cause for celebration, enough meat to keep a family alive and hopeful.

One of my grandmother's uncles was a *Pacífico* (a Peaceful One), who kept farming in order to feed his little brother. Another uncle was a blond man of primarily Spanish descent who married the daughter of a Congolese slave. My mother remembers seeing this couple coming into town with wild mountain flowers to sell. She says they were two of the happiest people she had ever seen. I like to picture them in love with each other, and with the beauty of their homeland, free of hatred, and free of war—free, in every sense of that short, powerful word. During a recent trip to Cuba, I met my mother's cousin Milagros, one of their descendants, whose name means "Miracles."

I feel privileged to have known my grandmother, who pressed wet sage leaves against her forehead whenever she had a headache, and my great-grandmother, who was young during Cuba's wars for independence from Spain, and Milagros, whose children are young and hopeful now.

Historical Note

In this story, Silvia and the oxcart driver are the only completely fictional characters. Their experiences are based on composites of accounts by various survivors of Weyler's reconcentration camps.

All the other characters are historical figures, including Rosario Castellanos Castellanos, known in Cuba as Rosa *la Bayamesa,* and her husband, José Francisco Varona, who helped establish and protect Rosa's hospitals. Some of the hospitals were mobile units, moving with the rebel *mambí* army. Others were thatched huts, hidden in the forest. Some were caves.

So little is known about the daily routines of Rosa and José that I have taken great liberties in imagining their actions, feelings, and thoughts.

Like many traditional Latin American healers, Rosa regarded healing as a gift from God and never accepted payment for her work as a nurse. Her medicines were made from wild plants. Many of these herbal remedies are still used in Cuba, where they are called *la medicina verde* (the green medicine).

Various accounts show Rosa's birth year as either 1834 or 1840. When she died on September 25, 1907, she was buried with full military honors. Her funeral was attended by a colonel of the U.S. Infantry's 17th Regiment.

There really was a slavehunter known as Lieutenant Death, but there is no evidence that he was the key figure in Spanish military operations designed to pursue and kill Rosa.

Other characters, such as *El Grillo* (The Cricket), *El Jóven* (The Young One), and *Las Hermanas de la Sombra* (The Sisters of Shade), are based on descriptions in the diaries of soldiers and war correspondents.

The first modern, systematic use of concentration camps as a way of controlling rural civilian populations was ordered by Imperial Spain's Captain-General Weyler in Cuba in 1896. No provisions were made for shelter, food, medicine, or sanitation. Estimates of the number of Cuban *guajiros* (peasants) who died in Weyler's "reconcentration camps" range from 170,000 to half a million, or approximately 10 to 30 percent of the island's total population. In some areas, up to 96 percent of the farms were destroyed.

After Spain ceded Cuba to the United States, Captain-General Weyler was promoted to Minister of War.

Within a few years, the ruthless military use of concentration camps was repeated during South Africa's Boer Wars. Adolf Hitler carried the genocidal concept to its extreme during World War II, when millions of European Jews, Catholics, gypsies, pacifists, and other minority groups were killed in Nazi Germany's extermination camps. Since then, armed powers all over the world have herded huge numbers of civilians into prison camps on the basis of religion, race, national origin, ideology, sexual orientation, style of dress, listening to rock music (Cuba's *roqueros*), or simply to seize territory, preventing farmers from growing crops that might strengthen an opposing army.

Cuba's third War of Independence from Spain is known in the United States as the Spanish-American War, and in Spain as *El Desastre* (The Disaster). Historians generally regard it as the first jungle guerrilla war, the first modern trench warfare, and the first time women were formally recognized as military nurses, both in the Cuban Army of Liberation and in the U.S. Army.

It is also known as the "journalist's war," because reporters working for American newspapers wrote stories promoting U.S. intervention. In 1897, when the renowned artist Frederic Remington requested permission to leave Cuba because he found the situation near

Havana reasonably quiet and unworthy of constant news coverage, his employer, William Randolph Hearst, owner of the *New York Morning Journal,* sent him an urgent telegram: "Please remain. You furnish the pictures. I'll furnish the war."

Chronology

EARLY INDEPENDENCE MOVEMENTS

1810. Cuba's first separatist movement is suppressed by colonial Spain.

1812. A slave rebellion is suppressed.

1823. *Soles y Rayos de Bolívar* (Suns and Rays of Bolívar) movement is suppressed, during a time when most other Spanish colonies have recently gained independence under the leadership of Simón Bolívar and other freedom fighters.

1836–55. Various separatist movements are suppressed.

1858–59. U.S. President James Buchanan makes offers to buy Cuba. Spain refuses.

1868. On October 10, Carlos Manuel de Céspedes and other landowners near the city of Bayamo in eastern Cuba burn their plantations and free their slaves, launching the first of three wars for independence from Spain.

1868–78. Cuba engages in its Ten Years' War for independence from Spain.

1878–80. Cuba fights its Little War for independence from Spain.

1880–86. Gradual abolition of slavery occurs throughout Cuba.

CUBA'S FINAL WAR FOR INDEPENDENCE
FROM SPAIN

1895. Rebellion in eastern Cuba begins. Poet José Martí is killed in his first battle.

1896. War spreads. Captain-General Weyler announces the reconcentration camp order.

1897. The Constitutional Assembly convenes.

1898. U.S. battleship *Maine* explodes in Havana Harbor. The United States makes its final offer to buy Cuba. U.S. military intervenes and Spanish troops surrender to U.S. troops. Cuban generals are not permitted to attend the ceremonies.

POSTWAR EVENTS

1899. Spain cedes rule of Cuba to the United States.

1902. The United States grants autonomy to Cuba, on the condition that U.S. troops retain the right to intervene in Cuban affairs and that Cuba allows a portion of the eastern province of Guantánamo to become a U.S. Navy base.

Selected References

ALLEN, DOUGLAS. *Frederic Remington and the Spanish-American War.* New York: Crown, 1971.

BARBOUR, THOMAS. *A Naturalist in Cuba.* Boston: Little, Brown and Company, 1946.

CORZO, GABINO DE LA ROSA. *Runaway Slave Settlements in Cuba.* Chapel Hill: University of North Carolina Press, 2003.

GARCÍA, FAUSTINO. *La Mujer Cubana en la Revolución.* La Habana: Bohemia, February 24, 1950.

GARCÍA, LUIS NAVARRO. *La Independencia de Cuba.* Madrid: Editorial MAPFRE, 1992.

GOLDSTEIN, DONALD M., AND KATHERINE V. DILLON. *The Spanish-American War—The Story and Photographs.* Washington, D.C., and London: Brassey's, 2000.

GÓMEZ, MÁXIMO. *Diario de Campaña del Mayor General Máximo Gómez.* La Habana: Comisión del Archivo de Máximo Gómez; Talleres del Centro Superior Tecnológico Ceiba del Agua, 1940.

MARTÍ, JOSÉ. *Poesía Completa.* La Habana: Editorial
Letras Cubanas, 1993.

PRADOS-TERREIRA, TERESA. Mambisas: *Rebel Women
in Nineteenth-Century Cuba.* Gainesville: University
Press of Florida, 2005.

ROIG, JUAN TOMÁS. *Plantas Medicinales, Aromáticas o
Venenosas de Cuba.* La Habana: Editorial Científico-
Técnica, 1988.

ROOSEVELT, THEODORE. *The Rough Riders.* New York:
Charles Scribner's Sons, 1899.

TONE, JOHN LAWRENCE. *War and Genocide in Cuba—
1895–1898.* Chapel Hill: The University of North
Carolina Press, 2006.

VILLAVERDE, CIRILO. *Diario del Rancheador.* La
Habana: Editorial Letras Cubanas, 1982.

Acknowledgments

I am deeply grateful to God and my family for the time and peace of mind to write.

For help with research, I am thankful to all the hard-working, anonymous interlibrary loan specialists from numerous libraries, including the Hispanic Reference Team at the Library of Congress.

A heartfelt thanks to my editor, Reka Simonsen, and to everyone else at Henry Holt and Company, especially Robin Tordini, Timothy Jones, my copy editor Marlene Tungseth and designer Lilian Rosenstreich.

For encouragement, I am grateful to Angelica Carpenter and Denise Sciandra at the Arne Nixon Center for Children's Literature, California State University, Fresno, and to Alma Flor Ada, Nancy Osa, Teresa Dovalpage, Juan Felipe Herrera, Anilú Bernardo, Cindy Wathen, Esmeralda Santiago, Midori Snyder, and Ellen Olinger.